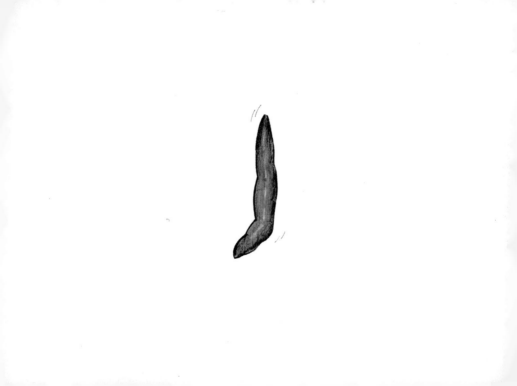

First published in 1989 by
Peter Hammer Verlag GmbH.

First published in the UK by
David Bennett Books, an imprint of Chrysalis Books plc,
64 Brewery Road, London N7 9NT

A member of Chrysalis Books plc

This small format edition first published in 2001
Reprinted 2001 and 2002

BRITISH LIBRARY
CATALOGUING-IN-PUBLICATION DATA
A catalogue record for this book is available
from the British Library.

ISBN 1 85602 440 7

Printed in China.

Werner Holzwarth / Wolf Erlbruch

FLora

The Story of the Little Mole
who knew it was None of his Business

David Bennett
BOOKS LIMITED

One day, the little Mole poked his head out from underground to see whether the sun had already risen. Then it happened!

It looked a little like a sausage, and the worst thing was that it landed right on his head.

"Did you do this on my head?" he asked the dove, who was flying past.

"Did you do this on my head?"
he asked the goat (who
had been dreaming
a little).

"Me? No, how could I? I do it like this!" she replied.

(And plippety plop — a pile of toffee-coloured little balls tumbled on the grass. The little mole found them almost appealing.)

"Did you do this on my head?"
he asked the cow, who was
chewing the cud.

Me? No, how could I?
I do it like this!"

And kersplosh — a big brownish-green
pancake flopped into the grass
just next to the mole. He was very
relieved that it hadn't been the cow
who had done something on his head.

"Did you do this on my head?"
he asked the pig.

"Me? No, how could I? I do it like this!" replied the pig.

(And plop, splat — a little, soft brown pile fell on to the grass. The mole held his nose.)

"Did you do this on my...?" he was going to ask again. But as he came closer, he saw only two big, fat, black flies. And they were eating. "At last — someone who will be able to help me!" thought the mole. "Who did this on my head?" he asked excitedly.

"Keep nice and still,"
buzzed the flies.
There was a short
pause. And then:
"It is clear to us that
it was A DOG."

Finally the little mole
knew who had done
the business on his head—

BASIL,
the butcher's dog!

Quick as a flash,
he climbed on to
Basil's kennel...

(And pling - a tiny black sausage
landed right on top of the dog's
head.)

Satisfied at last, the little mole disappeared happily into his hole underground.

Look out for these other David Bennett paperbacks!

Bang on the Door™ Karen Duncan, Jackie Robb, Berny Stringle, Sam Stringle
'Outrageous and witty comedy classics.' *Books Magazine*
The Story of Amoeba ISBN 1 85602 384 2
The Story of Armadillo ISBN 1 85602 337 0
The Story of Bat ISBN 1 85602 316 8
The Story of Brain Cell ISBN 1 85602 319 2
The Story of Cat ISBN 1 85602 314 1
The Story of Dog ISBN 1 85602 315 X
The Story of Pea Brain ISBN 1 85602 383 4
The Story of Plankton ISBN 1 85602 336 2
The Story of Slug ISBN 1 85602 317 6
The Story of Spider ISBN 1 85602 318 4

Full Moon Soup Alastair Graham
'You can spend hours with this book and still not see everything.' *Books for Keeps*
ISBN 1 85602 071 1

Full Moon Afloat Alastair Graham
Join in the fun as the *SS Splendide* sets off on a cruise of a lifetime!
ISBN 1 85602 217 X

Kevin Saves the World Daniel Postgate
'The neat story of a boy who is good at nothing except making faces…
well-paced… and a comfort to non-achievers of any age.' *Independent on Sunday*
ISBN 1 85602 268 4